This book belongs to

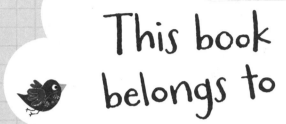

....

make
believe
ideas

Beauty
and the Beast

Key sound short e spellings:
a, ai, e, ea, ie, ue
Secondary sounds: ay, ea, th

Written by Rosie Greening
Illustrated by Clare Fennell

Reading with phonics

How to use this book

The **Reading with phonics** series helps you to have fun with your child and to support their learning of phonics and reading. It is aimed at children who have learned the letter sounds and are building confidence in their reading.

Each title in the series focuses on a different key sound or blend of sounds. The entertaining retelling of the story repeats this sound frequently, and the different spellings for the sound or blend of sounds are highlighted in red type. The first activity at the back of the book provides practice in reading and using words containing this sound or blend of sounds. The key sound for **Beauty and the Beast** is short e.

Start by reading the story to your child, asking them to join in with the refrain in bold. Next, encourage them to read the story with you. Give them a hand to decode tricky words.

Now look at the activity pages at the back of the book. These are intended for you and your child to enjoy together. Most are not activities to complete in pencil or pen, but by reading and talking or pointing.

The **Key sound** pages focus on one sound, and on the various different groups of letters that produce that sound. Encourage your child to read the different letter groups and complete the activity, so they become more aware of the variety of spellings there are for the same sound.

The **Letters together** pages look at three pairs or groups of letters and at the sounds they make as they work together. Help your child to read the words and trace the route on the word maps.

Rhyme is used a lot in these retellings. Whatever stage your child has reached in their learning of phonics, it is always good practice for them to listen carefully for sounds and find words that rhyme. The pages on **Rhyming words** take six words from the story and ask children to read and find other words that rhyme with them.

The **Key words** pages focus on a number of key words that occur regularly but can nonetheless be challenging. Many of these words are not sounded out following the rules of phonics and the easiest thing is for children to learn them by sight, so that they do not worry about decoding them. These pages encourage children to retell the story, practising key words as they do so.

The **Picture dictionary** page asks children to focus closely on nine words from the story. Encourage children to look carefully at each word, cover it with their hand, write it on a separate piece of paper, and finally, check it!

Do not complete all the activities at once – doing one each time you read will ensure that your child continues to enjoy the stories and the time you are spending together. **Have fun!**

King Fred was vain – he loved his looks!
He had no time for friends or books.
Instead, he liked to dance and sing:
"I am the world's best-looking king!"

But when one day Fred gave this cry,
Witch Wendy heard him from nearby.
"How vain he is!" Witch Wendy said.
"I think I'd better test King Fred."

Vain King Fred thinks he's the best.
Witch Wendy puts him to the test.

The clever witch disguised her face,
and then she went to King Fred's place.
She knocked upon the door and cried,
"Hey Fred, please let me step inside!"

But Fred just laughed and said, "Stay out!
You're ugly, like a Brussels sprout."
"Oh dear," said Wendy to the King:
"You know, good looks aren't everything."

Vain King Fred thinks he's the best.
The friendly witch is not impressed.

So Wendy waved her wand at Fred.
"I'm going to help you learn!" she said.
"A dreadful, ugly beast you'll be,
until you're free of vanity."

King Fred grew horns and bushy hair,
with claws just like a grizzly bear!
"I'm gross!" the beast yelled in disgrace,
and leapt inside to hide his face.

**Vain King Fred thinks he's the best.
His fur is like a messy nest!**

9

For several weeks, Beast stayed indoors
to hide his ugly face and claws.
He said, "I'm bored, and lonely too.
Without my looks, what will I do?"

Beast tried to paint,
but made a mess.

He had no guests
to play at chess.

"If I had any friends," he said,
"they'd keep me company instead."

**Vain King Fred thinks he's the best.
He's very lonely and distressed.**

That afternoon, at half past four,
a girl called Belle knocked on the door.
The tetchy beast stepped out and scowled.
"You're trespassing, you know!" he growled.

Young Belle was scared, but still polite –
she wouldn't leave without a fight!
"Hello," she said, "I'm selling books,
so would you like to take a look?"

Vain King Fred thinks he's the best.
The beast has got a special guest.

13

"A book might pass the time!" Beast said,
and let Belle step inside instead.
She spread the books out with a grin,
then said to Beast, "Now let's begin!"

The pair read many special tales,
with emperors, elves and friendly whales.
And by the time they reached the end,
the pair felt like the best of friends!

Vain King Fred thinks he's the best.
They have a friendly reading fest!

Thought Beast (as he set down his books),
"Belle's kind to me, despite my looks.
But when the witch knocked on my door,
her ugly face was all I saw."

He said, "How terrible I've been!
I need to be less vain and mean.
I'd rather have a friend and books
than be alone, with handsome looks."

King Fred no longer thinks he's best.
He tells himself, "I've been a pest!"

So Beast thought he would find a way
to thank Belle for their lovely day.
He found a giant, empty hall
with lots of bookshelves, standing tall.

He said to Belle, "Please close your eyes."
Then led her in and yelled, "Surprise!
As thanks for being kind to me,
I'm giving you a library!"

King Fred no longer thinks he's best.
But he is kinder than the rest!

The pair filled every shelf with care,
until new books were everywhere.
Then in a flash, and with a boom,
the witch appeared inside the room.

"You've learnt your lesson," Wendy said.
"Now you're not vain, but nice instead!
And since you gave this gift to Belle,
you're cured of selfishness as well."

King Fred no longer thinks he's best.
He has passed Witch Wendy's test!

Then with some sparks of gold and red,
the beast turned into handsome Fred.
The King proposed to Belle that day,
and they were wed without delay!

King Fred was lovely from then on –
his days of being mean were gone.
He never thought about his looks,
and kept his head inside his books!

King Fred no longer thinks he's best.
And no one ever would have guessed!

Key sound

There are several different groups of letters that make the short e sound. Practise them by following the books to help Beast tidy the library.

spread

red

Fred

read

instead

best

Wendy

rest

let

test

step

Letters together

Look at these pairs of letters and say the sounds they make.

ea   **ay**   **th**

Follow the words containing **ea** to turn Fred into a beast.

	ea	**grin**
leave	**in**	
		tales
please	**look**	**beast**
girl	**mean**	**four**

Follow the words containing **ay** to help Witch Wendy save the day.

ay

step

had

said

way

say

take

out

day

Follow the words containing **th** to thank Belle.

this

th

then

the

would

care

four

with

thank

27

Rhyming words

Read and say the words in the flowers, and then point to other words that rhyme with them.

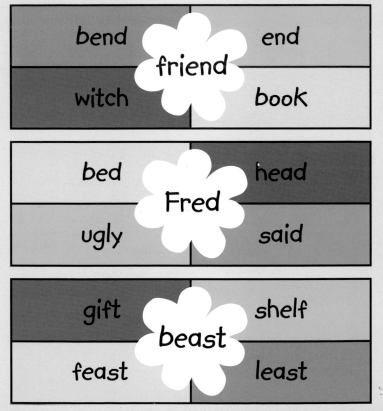

| bend | **friend** | end |
| witch | | book |

| bed | **Fred** | head |
| ugly | | said |

| gift | **beast** | shelf |
| feast | | least |

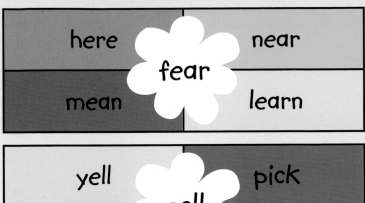

here	**fear**	near
mean		learn

yell	**sell**	pick
back		well

guest	**test**	stay
rest		best

Now choose a word and make up a rhyming chant!

Wendy **said**,
"I'll test King Fred!"
Fred **said**,
"Now I'm off to **bed**!"

Key words

Many common words can be tricky to sound out. Practise them by reading these sentences about the story. Now make more sentences using other key words from around the border.

King Fred **was** vain.

Witch Wendy played a trick **on** Fred.

She turned Fred into **a** beast.

not • your • mum • his • he

Beast **said**, "I feel lonely!"

• said • very • a • had • him • made • put • off • on •

A girl called Belle came **by**.

They read some books together.

Beast realised that he **had** been mean.

He gave Belle a library **for** her books.

The beast turned back **into** Fred.

King Fred got married **to** Belle.

her · saw · in · but · make · out · called · look · by · about · up · you · they · asked

old · see · like · into · for · with · was · to

Picture dictionary

Look carefully at the pictures and the words.
Now cover the words, one at a time.
Can you remember how to write them?

beast   books   claws

friend   horns   king

library   wand   witch